17

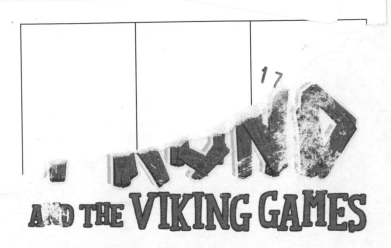

AND THE VIKING GAMES

First published 2014 by A & C Black
An imprint of Bloomsbury Publishing Plc
50 Bedford Square, London, WC1B 3DP

www.bloomsbury.com

Bloomsbury is a registered trademark of Bloomsbury Publishing Plc

ISBN 978-1-4729-0462-1

A CIP catalogue for this book is available from the British Library.

This book is produced using paper that is made from wood grown
in managed, sustainable forests. It is natural, renewable and
recyclable. The logging and manufacturing processes conform
to the environmental regulations of the country of origin.

Printed by CPI Group (UK) Ltd, Croydon CR0 4YY

1 3 5 7 9 10 8 6 4 2

LEIF FROND

AND THE VIKING GAMES

JOAN LENNON

Illustrated by
BRENDAN KEARNEY

A & C BLACK
AN IMPRINT OF BLOOMSBURY
LONDON   NEW DELHI   NEW YORK   SYDNEY

Contents

My name is Frond. Leif Frond. I'm ten years old and I'm a champion. I'm six foot tall, strong as a bear, with a big blond beard down to my waist...

All right, maybe not. Maybe not even five foot tall, and about as strong as a ferret. But just wait. It's going to happen. Any day now... any day...

My granny says things like, "You don't have to be as tall as a troll to make people sit up and take notice – look at your great-great-uncle, the one they called Gory Weaselbeard! Everybody knows about him and *he* was shorter than *me!*" I think she mustn't be telling the whole truth there, because my granny is so bent over she can look a sheep in the eye. And it's no secret that my great-great-uncle was the sneakiest trickster anyone has ever heard of and who wants to be known for *that*? Not me.

For me, it's champion or nothing.

CHAPTER ONE

Hosting the Games

"Thor's Elbow!" my father whispered, turning pasty pale. "It's her!"

We were standing on the shore, welcoming the visitors to the Midsummer Games. My father had just single-handedly carried four children and a tent to dry land yet now all the blood drained away from his face. He'd seen one last boat approaching – a boat flying the Hildefjord flag – a boat carrying...

...the Widow Brownhilde. Three words that

would strike terror into the heart of the greatest champion ever sung about by the bards.

Polite people called her 'a fine figure of a woman' and 'quite determined' but she was, in fact, *huge* and as relentless as a winter wolf. The Widow had used up three husbands already (first there was Knobbly Knerdman, then Bogboring the Yawn-maker and, last and least, Dogsdinner Dimson) and rumour had it she was on the prowl for Husband Four.

Rumour had it she had her eye on my father.

Did my father want to be Husband Four?

He very emphatically did *not*. And as far as *I* was concerned, having the Widow as my stepmother would be similar to getting savaged by wild pigs or swallowed whole by the World Serpent. At the same time.

"What am I going to do?" my father moaned under his breath. "Where can I hide? Is it my Fate to be bound to this horror?" I think he'd forgotten I was still there.

It was a cry for help if ever I heard one, and champions *never* ignore a cry for help.

"I'll save you, Father!" I said. I could see it already... Leif the Champion... Leif the Father-Saver... what wouldn't the bards give for a story like this! They would carry my fame to every settlement in the known world... I could see the little children and the women gathering round to hear the tale of my bravery, while all the men sat muttering enviously...

"Save me, mighty son of mine – save me from this terrible Fate!" Hallfred Frondfell looked down at the Champion with desperation like a cloak over his ageing shoulders...

(No, that wouldn't be right. It would be, he looked *up* at me, because *I* was the Champion and therefore the tallest person in the room. And I expect he wouldn't appreciate the 'ageing' crack.)

"Fear not, Still Fighting Fit Father," Leif the Tall and Handsome Champion cried. "I will

outwit this foul fiend or if needs must, I will slay her, and bring you her head on a platter."

"Well, that would be a bit extreme, even for the Widow Brownhilde," said my father. "But I appreciate the thought."

Rats! I really *have* to stop saying the things in my head out loud. "All right, all right, no head chopping. Not when we're hosting the Games. I can understand that. But, well, what I *can't* understand..."

My father sighed. "What can't you understand?"

"If you don't want to marry her, how can she *make* you?" I blurted out. "I mean, she's big, for sure, but you're bigger. You're stronger than her too. And you know how to use an axe and a javelin and a sword and all sorts of weapons. *She* can't do any of that."

My father sighed again, shaking his head. "None of that makes any difference. When a woman like the Widow makes up her mind, an army of trolls with an avalanche thrown in for good measure couldn't stop her getting what she wants. Still, anything you can do to keep me out of her clutches for as long as possible – *short* of chopping off her head – would be much appreciated." It was obvious he thought he was doomed. And he clearly didn't think there was anything much *I'd* be able to do about it.

Well, I was going to prove him wrong. A Viking Champion never ducks out of a challenge, no matter how horrifying.

"Of course I'll help you. I'll go right now and greet the Widow and show her where her men should set up their tents. I bet she'll want to supervise that – everybody knows how bossy she is – and in the meantime, *you* could go and check the games field, which is, as you know, on the other side of the settlement, right in the opposite direction."

"Perfect!" He was gone before you could

draw breath. A quick man, my father, in spite of him being the size of a moose.

Right, I thought. *Find the Widow, and head her off.*

There were visitors milling about everywhere, all dressed up and ready to have a good time, calling out greetings and exclaiming on how the children had grown and boasting about how well their young men would do this year at the Games. But even in such a crowd, it wasn't hard to find Brownhilde. I just made for the sound of someone giving a great long list of orders, loudly, who *wasn't* my sister Thorhalla (she's the one I'm pretty sure is part troll). And there she was – the utterly awful Widow. I walked right up to her, cleared my throat and said, "Welcome to Frondfell, ma'am."

"Eh? Is someone speaking to me?" she trumpeted. "I'm hearing voices!"

I sighed. "Down here, ma'am."

She still peered about for a moment before

she realised I was, in fact, in front of her, partially obscured by the major outcropping that was her bosom. I stepped out from under its shadow.

"Ah, there you are! Yes, boy? What do you want?"

"I have come to greet you, gracious lady, and offer you welcome to Frondfell. And escort you to a place for your people to put up your tents. And… and…" I stumbled to a halt. The Widow had bent over and was staring at me fixedly from scarily close quarters.

"I know those eyes," she muttered. Then, quick as a gannet, she grabbed my chin and tilted my head back and forth so hard I thought it might unscrew and come away in her hands. "You're Hallfred's boy, aren't you?"

I tried to nod. "Yes, ma'am. Hallfred Frond is my father."

It was a terrible mistake. The moment the words were out of my mouth, the Widow Brownhilde squealed with delight and then…

… she hugged me.

It was without a doubt the most appalling experience of my life.

She lifted me off the ground. It was like being smothered and, because she had big gold knobbly brooches on her dress, knobbled to death at the same time. It was horribly hot and… squirmy and… horrible and…

I don't want to talk about it.

Then, finally, just as I thought I was going to pass out from lack of air, the Widow dropped me. She was glaring at someone, and the look on her face could have soured milk that was still inside a cow.

The Widow had spotted Granny.

I don't know exactly where the bad blood between my granny and the Widow started. Nobody would tell me. As far as I can guess, one of them said something to the other one, and that one said something back, but it was all so awful that it can't be repeated to someone of tender years (by which they mean *me*).

There they stood, two tough-as-iron ladies, eyeballing each other. You'd be hard pressed to pick a clear favourite between them. The Widow had weight and reach but Granny – well, Granny had *cunning*.

It was going to be a long, long day.

But then something *else* happened, something which distracted me and Granny and the

Widow and everyone else on the beach as well. Did I say that the Widow's was the last ship to arrive? We'd all thought so, but we were wrong. Quite unexpectedly, *another* ship now came into view. And what a ship! It was magnificent, with an enormous red-and-white striped sail and a snarling dragon's head on its high prow and an array of battle-battered shields over more oarlocks than you could count. This was no ordinary boat. This was a raider – long, lean and fast, the kind of ship that strikes fear into coastal villages all over the known world.

But what was it doing at our Midsummer Games? All around me, people were asking each other the very same question, and nobody seemed to have the answer.

"Excuse me one moment," I said to the Widow Brownhilde.

And then I ran.

CHAPTER TWO

Champion of the Waves

There are pillaging-and-burning Vikings, and there are trading-and-fishing-and-farming Vikings. My family are the second kind, though most of my big brothers aren't completely happy about it. Even Karl, my nicest brother – well, he hasn't said anything, but I've watched how his eyes light up when the travelling bards come and recite the sagas, stories of adventure on the high seas, glorious battles and daring raids, and I know just how he feels.

My father says, "Sagas about death and destruction are all fine and good, but you can't trade with somebody if you've just slaughtered them."

You have to admit, he has a point.

But if my father is a trading-fishing-farming Viking, you only had to take one look at that longship to know that the people sailing in it *weren't*.

By the time I'd fetched my father back to the beach, the strangers were already dragging their ship up the shingle. Every last one of them had muscles trying to explode out of their skin and exotic scars and enough beard hair between them to blanket a mountain. But they were titchy compared to their leader.

He was gigantic, and he strode up our beach as if he owned it. He towered over even my father. He was wearing rich clothes and a fur cloak –

even though it was the middle of the summer – and he had the most magnificent ash blond beard I have ever seen. (I could see he thought it was pretty magnificent too, because he kept stroking it as if it were a cat.)

"Welcome to Frondfell," said my father. "And welcome to the Midsummer Games." There's no one on earth my father can't deal with (other than the Widow of course and, well, my granny) so I think it must have been the race to the beach that made his voice sound a little odd just then.

"Midsummer Games! Excellent!" the stranger bellowed. "Exactly what I need."

And then he just stood there, looking majestic and stroking his beard, surrounded by a sea of whispering, fidgeting folk, all in their festival finery, all bright-eyed and keyed-up.

"Who *is* he?" I hissed to my brother Karl.

"That's Harald Blogfeld!" Karl whispered back in a voice of deep awe.

"Who?"

"You don't know who Harald Blogfeld is?" Karl turned and stared down at me in amazement. "The Champion of the Waves? The Scourge of the Seas? The Viking's Viking? I heard he's the most successful raider there's ever been. I heard he attacks more villages in a season than anybody else!"

"*I* heard he's a nutter," said Thorhalla (my troll-sister), as she pushed by with a mead jug and a drinking horn, knocking me over as she went with a sly elbow.

"Shhh!" hissed Karl, horrified in case someone might have overheard what she'd said, but Thorhalla just tossed her braids at him. She went right up to the great man as if he were just another guest in a busy hostess's day, and poured him a welcoming drink. She didn't tremble or curtsey or anything. She's pretty hard-boiled, Thorhalla. Maybe it's the troll in her. Maybe if *I* had some troll blood in me, I'd be utterly fearless too. Of course, I'd also be utterly obnoxious, and champions are *never* obnoxious. Still, it would come in handy, not being scared of anything… they would call me Leif the Unafraid… Leif the –

"Leif! Stop muttering! Harald Blogfeld is about to speak!" Karl nudged me in the ribs so hard I fell over (again). He didn't mean anything by it, though – he's just really, really strong. And he helped me up afterwards.

Blogfeld was looking us all over with a calculating gleam in his eyes. "Well, you can count yourselves lucky this day, good folk," he boomed. (I could see people in the front rows swaying back at the force of the blast.) "Because I find myself in an unusual position. Here I am, all set to launch yet another astonishingly successful raiding season, scourging the seas, terrorizing the waves, when what do you know – I discover I'm a champion short! Yesterday, one of my best men broke his leg in a wrestling match with a bear."

"He wrestled a bear?" exclaimed my father.

Blogfeld shrugged. "It was a dare – what else could he do?"

Wrestle a bear?! I yipped inside my head. And yet, how could anyone who considered themselves a proper champion *not* accept a challenge like that? I've never actually met a bear close up, let alone approached one in a wrestling frame of mind, but if someone had *dared* me... as the man said, what else could I possibly do? I just hoped that nobody would ever think of setting me that particular test.

Blogfeld was still speaking. "Of course, my man begged me to let him come along anyway, despite the fact that he kept falling over in agony every time he tried to stand up, but I had to say no. There is no room for wussiness of any sort on my ship. Instead, I stopped off here, and what do I find?"

He paused, but none of us knew the answer to that. What *had* he found?

"The perfect recruiting ground," he explained. "A Midsummer Games! What could be better?"

There was a rustle of excitement in the crowd.

"I'm going to find the best, strongest, fiercest, bravest champion from among all the contestants from all the settlements gathered here today and offer him my bear-wrestler's place."

Suddenly every man in the crowd was standing up taller, chests puffed out, shoulders straightened.

"But how, you may wonder, will I know which of you is the best, strongest, fiercest and bravest?" Blogfeld went on. "Wonder no more – all I have to do is watch the Games and award the place to the one I think is the Overall Champion. Oh, and don't worry – my own men won't be competing. Well, I mean, just look at them! It would hardly be fair, would it?"

We all looked at them and their muscles and their scars. We all absolutely agreed.

"Enough talk – let the Games begin!"

concluded the Scourge of the Seas and, with that, he and his men strode up the beach, driving through the crowd like an axe through butter.

I turned to speak to Karl, but he was staring after Blogfeld with a goopy expression on his face – and then, so suddenly it made me yelp, he grabbed my arm.

"He's got to choose me!" he exclaimed, and his eyes were all crazy-looking. "Whatever it takes. I've got to win. I've *got* to!"

Then I yelped again because another, bony hand had grabbed my *other* arm.

It was my granny. She peered over me at Karl and said (very loudly), "Well, there's nothing to worry about there, lad. In fact, I'll just go and get your sleeping furs rolled up and ready to go, shall I?"

But then the ground trembled slightly and there was the Widow Brownhilde towering over Granny.

"Oh, you sweet, tiny, deluded little old lady!" the Widow half-simpered, half-snarled. "There's no need for you to hurry off and do any such thing. I'm sure your boy – Curly, is that his name? – is really quite good. Strong. Brave. Thoroughly lovely. But he won't have a chance of being chosen for a *man's* job like this one." Granny's lips thinned dangerously, but the Widow paid no attention. "It'll be someone from *my* settlement who'll be winning here today, rest assured."

"One of *your* lads?" snorted my granny, starting to go purple in the face. "From Hildefjord? Don't make me laugh."

Thor's Hangnail! I gulped. *This is going to get ugly!*

"Oh, look, now I've upset you," continued the Widow. "And I'm sure it's very bad for someone as really incredibly feeble and old as you to get over-excited. So, never you mind. I'm sure Cutey will do very nicely indeed."

"His name's Karl," hissed Granny.

"Of course, dear," said the Widow as she turned away. "Whatever you say."

"Karl – grab Granny!" I hissed and, fortunately, my brother managed to catch our grandmother just as she launched herself at Brownhilde's back in a creaky but determined tackle. Karl had no difficulty in holding on to her, though her little feet were peddling furiously in mid-air, and I wouldn't like to say what words she was mouthing at our guest.

"Is there a problem?" asked my father anxiously as he bustled up. "Only I really should be getting the Games star – arrggh! – ah, er…"

"*Hallfred*! Is that *you*?" trilled the Widow, whirling round. But my father was already trying to bury himself in the crowd.

Before Brownhilde could set off in pursuit, I rushed forward to intercept her. "This way, gracious lady, follow me. My father wants you to have the best seat. Hurry – the Games are about to begin!" Using every scrap of strength I could muster, I started to tow her in the opposite direction.

And all the while I was thinking, *Oh, great. Now I've got to keep the Widow away from my father, and my granny away from the Widow, and me away from all my sisters (but especially Thorhalla), and still find time to become a Champion in the Games.*

Some days you'd be better off never even getting out of bed.

CHAPTER THREE

Leif's Secret

"Just here, ma'am. This is the best place to see the first event. Right by the archery target. They'll be unveiling it any minute now." I was babbling, but I couldn't seem to stop. "You know, of course you do, how the Artificers of each settlement try to outdo the others in making the most spectacular archery target imaginable – and Queue the Frondfell Artificer is truly exceptional. Probably the best in the world. I just know you'll be impressed."

It was the wrong thing to say.

You wouldn't have thought it was *possible* for the Widow's bosom to get any larger, but she really did seem to expand with indignation. She was furious.

"Have you forgotten the amazing archery target the Hildefjord Artificers created only last summer?" she spluttered. (How could I have? It was shaped like a giant mead cup that was supposed to fountain up spectacularly with the winning shot. But every time one of the contestants hit it *anywhere*, it started to leak. Spectators kept running out onto the field to fill their own cups. It was all a bit of a disaster.) Then she deflated herself a little, and gave me a smile that made my blood run cold. "Still I think it's sweet that you're so young and yet so loyal. Such a dear little fellow."

Great Thor's Ankles! I cried silently. *She's going to do it again!*

All the signs were there, but before she could

actually execute her fiendish plan of once more hugging me, a loud trumpeting drifted across the fields, announcing that the first of the Games was about to begin.

Saved by the horn!

I gulped, and ran to fetch my bow.

Now, as I said before, I had a lot on my mind trying to keep the grown-ups under control, but right at that moment there was something else troubling me.

I don't know how to say this to make it sound good or even remotely heroic. That's probably because there *is* no way to make it sound anything but weaselly.

I was planning to cheat.

It's like this. The Midsummer Games had been looming large in everyone's minds – especially this year when it was being held here at Frondfell. My sisters were fussing about food; Granny was telling everybody exactly what would go wrong if they didn't do things her way; my brothers were all training like mad; Queue the Artificer was very busy and being close-mouthed about his archery target-building plans. (I asked him once why he was called Queue. "Why do you think?" he snorted. "It's because I'm so good, people have to queue up to see me!" And it's true. He really is very, very good.) And I... I was desperate to qualify to compete for the very first time – and there was only one way I could see to make it happen. After a lot of arguing inside my head I made up my mind. I went to Queue's workshop and after humming and hawing for ages, I came right out with it.

I asked him to make me a Magic Bow.

At first, Queue just looked at me for a long moment. Then, without saying a word, he went into the back of the workshop, where the shadows are mysterious and deep, and he brought back a bow.

"There you are," he said. "I just finished making it last week."

I couldn't believe it. I took the bow, feeling all
tingly and awed.

"How does the magic work?" I whispered.

Queue held up a finger. "You must never ask
questions about a Magic Bow," he rumbled.
"Now go away and learn how to use it."

"Thank you! Thank you!" I called over
my shoulder.

I'd been practising like crazy ever since last

year's Games, but now I redoubled my efforts. At first it didn't seem as if the Magic Bow made any difference at all, but then, gradually, I started to get better. And better. Until I was good enough to hit the test target and convince my father I was ready to compete. He looked so proud. I almost blurted it all out, all about my Magic Bow, all about being a cheater, but in the end, I didn't. And now...

Now here I was, lining up with the other contestants, clutching my Magic Bow so tightly my knuckles showed white. Everything seemed unnaturally bright and clear and shiny – the sky, the grass, the spectators lining the field in their festival clothes. I could see my granny rushing about with cups of mead for the contestants, which was odd since she usually left that sort of leg work to my sisters (who usually passed it on to me). I thought she might have taken a break to cheer for me, this being my first Games and all, but there was no time left to worry about that now. My father gave the signal to Queue. There was a dramatic pause, and then our Artificer pulled away the sheet with a flourish and the Frondfell archery target was revealed.

Everyone gasped. It was *stupendous*.

CHAPTER FOUR

Fate's Arrow

It was a monstrous demon boar.

If you looked really closely, you could see that it actually was a wooden frame, bulked out with bales of straw and cunningly covered with cloth painted to look like rough hide and curved tusks and tiny piggy red eyes. But I'm willing to bet there wasn't a single archer there who thought about it that way. It was as if we'd fallen into the middle of a great saga. Here we stood – a line of champions – and there was the beast that must be slain.

The first archer notched his arrow.

"I will aim for the throat, for that is the way to kill a demon boar!" he cried. The crowd muttered agreement. But when his arrow pierced the boar in the throat, nothing happened.

"Everyone knows you must aim for the heart," cried the next, "however small that might be." The crowd agreed with that too. But the monster's heart must have been smaller than my sister Thorhalla's, for though many arrows clustered in the target's chest, none of them seemed able to find it.

"I will pierce its hump!"

"I will shoot its tusk!"

They all thought they knew best. But none of the arrows had any effect. The winning shot was supposed to make something *happen*. Artificers up and down the coast put huge effort into building targets every year – the competition to create the newest and most spectacular was fierce – but the answer to where the winning arrow needed to go was always a deep secret.

When it was my brother Karl's turn, he didn't boast or shout about what he was going to do. He just walked up to the mark, drew his bow, aimed, and let fly.

Everyone spontaneously cheered. Karl's arrow was clearly visible. It had flown straight and true – and had pierced the boar target's tiny eye!

It was an amazing shot and yet – there was *still* no sign of any reaction from the beast of straw.

There were murmurs all around.

"If anything could kill a monster it'd be an arrow to the eye."

"No one can beat a shot like that!"

"This isn't as much fun as the Hildefjord archery target – I think the thing's broken."

I hope Queue didn't hear that, I thought to myself and then I looked around and realised with horror that there was only one person left to shoot…

Me. The cheater with the Magic Bow.

I didn't know *what* to do. My stomach was trying to crawl up into my throat and I kept waiting for someone in the crowd to shout out, "Hey! Look at that! That boy's cheating – he's got a Magic Bow!" And then they'd boo. And throw things. Viking crowds like throwing things. Squishy vegetables and elderly fruit for preference. (Well, rocks and knives for preference, but not at a festival.) Getting pelted with old apples and over-ripe cabbage – what kind of Fate was that for a champion?

And that was when it hit me – not a turnip, but the answer. Fate! I'd been playing fast and loose with the rules, taking them into my own hands, and now it was time for me to hand them back.

I would leave it all up to Fate.

Suddenly my nervousness left me and I almost smiled. I pointed the bow in the general vicinity

of the target, pulled back the string, and shut my eyes.

Whush – Sproingg!

"*Look!*" cried the crowd, so of course I opened my eyes again.

It was an astonishing sight.

There was my arrow, in plain view, stuck right in the monster boar's bottom. And, where all other arrows had failed to set off the target's mechanism, mine had, against all the odds, succeeded.

There was a grating and a grinding and a shuddering, and the boar began to twitch and jerk. Slowly, terrifyingly, it raised its head and then, so suddenly it made everybody jump, it spat flame from its mouth. Right up into the sky, a great torch of fire and smoke. And my shot had set it off – not only my bow, but my *arrow* must have been magic as well!

And the crowd roared. Even the spectators nearest the target who were now thoroughly covered in soot – including the Widow Brownhilde – choked and cheered. But not all of the contestants were happy. Archers with far greater skill than mine had hit the target in far more difficult and, let's face it, more *heroic* places.

"My arrow pierced its *heart*," muttered one.

"*My* arrow pierced it straight through the throat," grumbled another.

"Have you ever tried to shoot a boar's tusk?" complained a third.

Queue came trotting up, breathless and soot-stained and grinning like mad. He was immediately bombarded with protests from the unsuccessful competitors.

"You can't kill a boar by sticking an arrow in its bottom," one cried.

"Maybe not, but you can probably get him angry enough to spit flames." Queue replied. He was looking very pleased with himself.

"You never told us *that* was what we were after!" protested another red-faced archer.

"Everybody thought we were supposed to kill the thing," spluttered a third.

"Well, he's not looking too well now, wouldn't you agree?" said Queue cheerfully. That got a laugh from the crowd – and he was absolutely right. While they had been arguing, the entire straw construction had caught fire. The target was now a mass of flame and, as we all watched, it toppled slowly over onto its side.

"Looks dead to me," said Queue.

"I… you're right, but… um …" stuttered my father. His job as host of the Frondfell Midsummer Games was proving exceptionally difficult.

But Blogfeld, the Scourge of the Seas, couldn't stop laughing. *He* seemed to be having a wonderful time.

"That young fellow is the only one among you who got to the bottom of it all!" he hooted in his ocean-going voice. "Get it? The bottom? Get it?"

"But still… it was hardly the *best* shot," murmured my father.

"You're right. I can't argue with that. I'd say the eye-shooter wins this one. But I insist we give the young fellow some credit anyway! And of course your Artificer – that was a spectacular display! I wonder how he did it?"

Well, nobody was going to argue out loud with Harald Blogfeld. (That didn't mean there weren't grumblers, because there always are. And it didn't mean the whole thing wouldn't be relived and torn apart and put back together a dozen different ways before the next Midsummer Games, because that always happened too.)

So the decision was announced that Karl's had been the winning shot. And you know, I was relieved. I hadn't won fair and square, and no amount of smoke and fire could make it otherwise. We could still hear Blogfeld, though, chortling and repeating, "He got to the bottom of it, didn't he, that boy? The bottom!"

"Ooo, I do love a man with a sense of humour!" my granny cackled suddenly. (You never hear my granny coming – she's just all of a sudden *there*, at your elbow.) She had another cup of mead in her hands, but she wouldn't let me have any. "No, you can't have this – it's for that awful – I mean that *lovely* woman Brownhilde. Where *is* she?"

My heart sank. "Granny, what's in that cup?"

"What, this cup? Why, it's a mead cup, you silly boy. It's got mead in it – you know, honey and water and, er, things."

"What kind of things?" I said sternly.

"Just… a little medicine. It's special. I've been giving it to as many of our guests as I can. Especially the ones from Hildefjord. It's gone down really well."

"What *kind* of medicine?"

"Well, let's just say, there'll be a lot of visitors to the latrines for the next few hours. I guess *they'll* be getting to the bottom of things as well!" And she snuffled and snorted at her own joke for a ridiculously long time. I waited until she finally stopped.

"Granny," I said.

"Yes?"

"Give me the cup."

I thought for a moment she was going to argue, but then she just shrugged and handed it over. I poured the contents out onto the grass. "And you're not to make any more," I added.

"Can't anyway," she said. "No more of the special ingredient left." There wasn't a trace of remorse in her voice. But I couldn't really scold her. Not when I was holding my own guilty secret right there in my hand.

Without another word, I left my granny. I walked over to Queue and held out the bow he'd given me.

"Here," I said. "Please take back your Magic Bow. I was wrong to have asked for it in the first place."

But the Artificer didn't take it back. "That bow isn't magic, you silly boy," he said gruffly.

I stared. "But you told me... You said..."

Queue shrugged. He was looking a little embarrassed, which was unusual for him. "Look, it was your first Games. I told you what I thought would calm you down. Nobody shoots their best when they're all fussed and twitchy."

"But... but..." I spluttered. "I was the one who hit the right place. On the target. I was the one who made the boar flame."

"*That* wasn't magic," grunted Queue.

"Well, what was it then?" I squeaked.

"That? Oh, that was just Fate!" And with a nod, the Artificer turned on his heel and walked away.

CHAPTER FIVE

The Rough and the (Very) Smooth

Now, the thing about Viking Games is – they can get a bit rough. Well, actually, they can get *very* rough. And the roughest event of all is the wrestling. In a normal match you can confidently expect damage to be done to one or both of the contestants. And with the prize of a place in Blogfeld's ship for the season dangling before them, the young men obviously thought this wasn't the day to start being delicate with each other. That (and Granny's laxative-laced mead) was having a big impact on the number of casualties.

My sisters were up to their eyeballs in wounded contestants and it was only by shifting ground constantly that I managed to avoid having to help them dust the losers down and patch them up. I hadn't time for anything like that – *I* had to keep my eyes on the *unofficial* contestants.

Where were they all? As I skirted the edge of the wrestling ring I could see my father, with Blogfeld beside him. And powering up the hill towards them both, I could also see the Widow. (She'd obviously been making use of our bathhouse to wash off the worst of the soot from Queue's target, and she was still dripping round the edges.) There was a predatory gleam in her eyes as she parted the crowd the way the prow of a ship parts the waves.

I had to head her off.

Have you ever had one of those nightmares where you want to run but your legs go all treacle-y? This was exactly like that. I tried my hardest to push past all the people but I couldn't get them to let me through. I poked and pinched and elbowed and got precisely nowhere. It was only when I dropped to my hands and knees and started *crawling* through the crowd that I made some headway.

Unfortunately it was while I was doing that, down on all fours, that my path and the Widow's converged.

It was like a mighty oak toppling over in the forest, only with added screeching.

I watched, helpless, terrified the Widow would crush the life out of any poor soul she landed on. Even my father wouldn't have been able to withstand the equivalent of half a mountain falling on top of him. But there was one man there that day who could – and luckily for the

Widow, that was the man who caught her. Harald Blogfeld gave a great grunt and his knees buckled with the effort of breaking her fall, but he didn't let her hit the ground.

"Oh. Oh! Thank you, kind sir," simpered the Widow as he hauled her upright again.

"Nnnn... nurgle... er..." The Champion of the Waves seemed oddly tongue-tied, but that was probably because he'd just had all the breath forcibly knocked out of him.

I staggered to my feet, grabbed my father by the arm and dragged him away from the giant couple.

"Thanks, lad!" murmured my father. "Now just see what your granny's up to, would you? You know what she's like about the wrestling!"

I did know.

She wasn't hard to find. There she was, as I'd expected, right at the front. Granny is *always* in the front row at wrestling matches. The fact is, she's not so much interested in wrestling as she is in commenting on how the contestants look in just their shorts. As each pair of young men came into the ring she got louder and louder.

"Would you just look at those muscles?! Ooo, come on gorgeous give us a ripple! My, he does strip off nicely, doesn't he? His father had a lovely body too, as I remember…"

I kept trying to shush her but it didn't work. Everyone else roared with laughter, which, of course, only encouraged her. It was just entertainment to them, but I'm *related*! The more I shushed, the more outrageous she got.

You'd almost think she *enjoyed* embarrassing me.

The match everyone was looking forward to most was the one between my brother Karl and Hildefjord's best contestant, Manni. In spite of the fact that he came from the Widow's settlement, Manni was a really nice person – and an excellent wrestler. They were scheduled last, as a sort of star event.

Manni rippled his muscles at my brother and called out with a broad smile. "Don't look so scared – I promise I won't hurt you... much."

"Brave words, little man." Karl grinned back at him. "Brave..."

But just then a peculiar expression came over my brother's face. He turned pale. Then he turned red.

"I..." he said in a strangled sort of voice. "I... um..." And suddenly he was gone, racing for the latrines.

"Granny!" I hissed.

"Someone must have shared their cup with him," she whispered back defensively. "What, do you think I'd give it to him deliberately?"

There was a pause as the crowd exchanged puzzled glances.

"Um... there seems to be a lot of that going around," said my father wearily.

"I'm happy to wrestle someone else, sir," said Manni politely.

"That's very decent of you," said my father. "But apparently there have been a number of disqualifications and we, um, we appear to have run out of competitors."

The Widow had already stepped forward to congratulate *her* contestant on being the winner by default, when…

"Not quite!" shrilled Granny.

"What?" said my father. He looked pained, as if he were getting a headache.

"You're not quite out of contestants," said Granny.

I looked about, relieved. Who had shown up? Was it Brand? Or Haki? Not either of the twins, I hoped. They were both useless at wrestling. Who was she talking about?

"Just give me a moment to strip him down, and he's all yours," called Granny. And then, for no reason that I could see, she grabbed me by the sleeve and dragged me away in the direction of the Hall.

"Wha... what?!"

"It's you or nobody," she grunted. "Now get your shirt off."

I could not believe what was happening. I tried to pull away.

"What about Haki? Or the twins? Or – "

"Haven't you been paying attention? Haki's sprained his wrist, Brand's wrenched his shoulder, and the twins have been disqualified for trying to nobble some of the Hildefjord wrestlers before the event." Granny snorted. "I wouldn't mind them having a go, if they'd been any good at it. But they weren't. So, undress yourself *now* – or I'll do it for you!" she said, as we arrived in the Hall.

Reluctantly, I started to pull my shirt over my head, thinking all the while, *Manni is going to massacre me. My entire body's about as thick as one of his arms. Why does my granny hate me all of a sudden?* Then, as I emerged, it got worse. She had a pot of something horrible and stinky in her hands, and a strange gleam in her eyes.

"What's that smell? *Hey!*" I squealed.

"Stop wriggling," my granny scolded, as she rubbed great globs of the foul-smelling stuff onto me. "It's my best quality goose-fat ache ointment."

"But I'm not sore!" I cried, trying to squirm out of her bony grip.

"You will be," she muttered, not letting go at all. "You will be."

And then, after checking that I was entirely basted in ointment, she herded me outside, and back to the wrestling ring.

Have I mentioned I'm not exactly fully-grown yet? That might not give you a completely clear picture. Think shoulders of a ferret, arms of a plucked chicken and the overall physique of a rat in a lean year, and you'll understand that stripping me down to my shorts is not the way to see me at my best. But, there I was in the wrestling ring, *being* seen by everyone I have ever known and quite a few strangers besides.

It was a nightmare in the daytime.

Basically, I could barely move for embarrassment, and it could have all ended right then and there, if it hadn't been for my granny's stick, which has quite a sharp pointy end, and which she unexpectedly poked my bottom with.

I lunged forward with a sort of stifled war cry. Manni assumed I was attacking and grabbed at me – and I scooted straight out of his hands and across to the other side of the ring.

"What?" both Manni and I exclaimed.

There was a moment of stunned silence in the crowd, and then...

"Bet he can't do *that* twice!" crowed someone.

"I'll take that bet!" yelled someone else – and then *he* gave me a shove, sending me right back at Manni with a flying leap.

And it happened again. As I slithered wildly

out of his grip all I could see was the astonished look on his face. He'd never had an opponent like me before!

The crowd called out for more. Everyone was laughing – but they were cheering too. Before anybody else could 'help', I dove back into the fray and slid wildly across Manni's chest as he tried to grab hold of me and completely failed. Granny's goose-fat ointment had turned me into something utterly ungrippable.

"It's like watching a big old bear trying to catch a salmon!" I heard someone say above the laughter and applause.

I'm an uncatchable fish! I was starting to get excited. Could there possibly be some way of turning this whole embarrassing episode into something worthy of a real champion?

I turned for another go, and then I noticed that Manni had started to wheeze weirdly. He began to stagger. Was this my chance? I flung myself at him one more time, slid off at an angle, landed on my feet, and turned just in time to see him crash to the ground.

Abruptly, the crowd fell silent. Manni was shaking and twitching and making a strange noise. What had I done? Was he having a heart attack? I know the sagas talk about men making their first kill when they're only young, but... but... Manni was *nice*...

"Manni? Manni! Are you all right?" I rushed over to him, completely forgetting that this might well be a trick to get me within arm's reach. But there was nothing here that seemed like a ruse. He was breathing in great gulps, and there were tears streaming from his eyes, and he was clutching his stomach.

"Oh, Manni – I'm so sorry – I –"

Then my father hurried into the ring and pushed me to one side. He knelt down and began to examine my fallen opponent for broken bones or internal injury. My heart was twisting in my chest like a hooked eel. The crowd was completely silent. Then my father slowly stood up. He had a peculiar expression on his face.

I grabbed his arm – I needed to know. "Tell me – is he going to be all right? Have I... *killed* him?" I felt really, really awful – and then I realised that things weren't quite the way they seemed.

Manni wasn't dying.

He was laughing.

He was rolling around on the ground, not in pain, but because he was crying, wheezing, hooting with hilarity. I had rendered my opponent helpless by being funnier than anything he'd ever come across in his whole life.

At that moment, I almost wished he *were* dying.

My father just stood there, looking from me to the still-giggling Manni and back to me again.

He didn't know what to do.

But the crowd did.

"The winner's Little Salmon!" they cried.

"Slippery Fish! Slippery Fish!"

"Best laugh I've had all year!"

It was too much for any grease-covered champion to face.

I turned tail, and ran.

CHAPTER SIX

Surprisingly Uplifting

But not even embarrassment could keep me away from the final event of the Games.

The weightlifting.

The rules for Viking weightlifting are simple. There is a big boulder. There is a track. Each contestant picks up the big boulder and sees how far they can carry it along the track. Perfectly straightforward.

But in these Games, *nothing* was straightforward. First Wandering Nell, our eccentric escape-mad cow, came blundering over to see what all the commotion was about. She managed to leave several large steamy cowpats on the track while I was trying to get her to go away again, and guess who got to clean *that* up?

Then there were the very different smells of the feast drifting distractingly down from the Hall. Sometimes this is where you can start to lose the crowd. But today, with Blogfeld about and all the weird happenings, nobody was going to risk missing out on anything, even for first dibs on the roast meat.

So, as we gathered down by the stream I wasn't surprised to see that there was an especially good crowd of spectators. However I couldn't help noticing there was also a definite – and worrying – shortage of contestants.

"Where is everyone?" wondered my father anxiously. He was standing by the weightlifting boulder. All in a cluster beside him were the Widow, Harald Blogfeld and my granny. It was impossible to separate that lot! And my granny had another one of those pleased-with-herself looks all over her face.

Oh-oh, I thought.

What on earth was she up to this time?

"Where *are* they?" my father repeated, peering about. "I really don't understand."

Then my granny spoke up.

"Oh, I was supposed to tell you all – quite a number of the young men said to start without them," she said in a clear, carrying voice. "They've all gone up the mountain for a while."

My father wearily closed his eyes.

"Why?" he asked.

"Oh, because I'm almost certain I saw an enormous eagle," my granny said innocently. "Circling over the Weirdly Crag. I told all the young men I met about it. I may have also mentioned how impressed we'd all be with the one who could catch such a bird to present to our honoured guest." She leered up at Harald

Blogfeld and I have a horrible feeling she may have winked. "I *know* you'd look ever so fine with an eagle on your fist," she said sweetly.

She was right. Blogfeld *would* look amazing with a huge bird like that. Anyone would! For a moment I could see *myself* with such a mighty creature...

... its tearing talons clasped with an iron grip on the leather guard the champion wore on his great right forearm, its cruel beak ever ready to rip and rend, its glinting golden eye staring into his, searching for signs of fear or weakness, searching in vain...

And then common sense kicked in, and I had to admit that a bird like that would probably weigh as much as I do, and trying to attach one to my arm would immediately tip me over onto my face.

"Well then, I suppose we'll have to call it a day," my father was saying. "If there is no one from any of the settlements willing to come forward and compete?"

It was a depressing end to our Games. We'd worked so hard to make them the best, and what with the special mead and the boar's bottom and the whole fiasco with me and the grease and then all the contestants disappearing on this wild-goose eagle chase, it had turned into a fizzle.

Then someone stepped up to the mark.

It was my granny.

"What are you doing *now*?" moaned my father.

"What does it look like? I'm entering the competition."

"But... why?"

"Why, for the honour of Frondfell! Look, I see it this way. If there's only one competitor, that competitor wins, am I right? And since I'm the only one here, that means I win. Frondfell, the host settlement, wins. I don't see how anyone can argue with that."

"But you... you haven't even picked up the boulder!" protested my father, a truly desperate note in his voice.

"Is that all?" said my granny. "Well, I'm happy to give it a go. How hard can it be?"

With one voice, my father and I groaned. With one voice, the crowd cheered! My granny, of course, listened to the crowd. She waved and grinned and then, first carefully laying down her stick, she spat on her hands, grabbed the boulder – which was not far off being as big as she was – and heaved.

Nothing happened.

My granny shifted her grip a little and heaved again.

And again nothing happened.

The crowd was willing her on, but my father had already stepped forward to put an end to it when the Widow Brownhilde did something truly amazing.

Very calmly, without any fuss, she walked over to where my granny was struggling with the boulder. She looked at her for a moment, then bent forward, wrapped her arms around

Granny *and* the boulder and, astonishingly, picked them both up. Without even a grunt or a groan she carried her burden right to the end of the track and then even further, on to the edge of the stream and then...

... *she dropped them in!*

Well, you have never heard language like that! My granny came to the surface spluttering and swearing and sopping wet. She was mad, all right. But, like a cat or a hen, old people can look a whole lot smaller and more fragile when you drench them, and I think the Widow must have got a shock when she saw just how tiny my granny looked, standing there up to her hips in the chilly water. Whatever the reason, Brownhilde leaned over and held out a hand.

"Here – I'll help you," she cried.

Big mistake, I thought, seeing the look on my granny's face. *Big, big mistake.*

I was right.

My granny looked at the hand that was being stretched out to her, and she looked at the way the Widow was a bit off balance, and she grabbed that hand with her bony old fingers and pulled.

The splash Brownhilde made as she hit the stream was colossal. When she rose up out of the water again it was like watching a breaching whale. Fearing she might be feeling rather lethal, my father rushed forward to rescue my granny and Harald Blogfeld went to rescue the Widow, and somehow they both managed to fall into the stream as well. And then all the spectators got involved, trying to rescue *them*, and then each other, and by the time the feast bell was rung, there were more soaking wet guests than dry ones, and everybody had great big grins plastered all over their faces.

The Viking Games had ended not with a bang, but with a splash, and we all headed with a good will towards the Hall and the feast.

CHAPTER SEVEN

But Who Won?

By midnight, even the greediest of our guests was starting to slow down. The young men who'd spent the last part of the day hunting Granny's imaginary eagle had returned. They were all full of tales about how close they'd come to trapping the bird and what hungry work it had been. They certainly did the Frondfell feast justice. (The ones who'd spent the same amount of time in the Frondfell latrines were a bit more careful.) My sisters were dragging themselves back and forth, continuing to serve the company with fixed smiles and gritted teeth. Why do visitors never seem to notice when it's time to call it a day? I leaned back against the wall and imagined how popular I would be if I were a magician. A *champion* magician who specialised in Go Home spells. I would rent myself out to anyone hosting a feast... I would be much sought after... treated with huge respect...

I opened my eyes, half expecting *our* Hall to be emptied of guests. But, of course, even a dozen magic spells wouldn't get anyone to budge until we'd heard the results of the day's competition – who was to become Harald Blogfeld's latest recruit?

But before we could find out the answer to that, we had to find out what had become of Harald Blogfeld. Nobody knew where he'd got to. And another thing – where was the Widow Brownhilde? She, too, seemed to be missing. It was very strange...

And then, the answer to our questions strolled in through the door.

Harald Blogfeld and the Widow Brownhilde, together!

There was a strange expression on the big man's face, and the Widow looked like the cat who's got at the cream. They were walking arm in arm.

At the sight of the Scourge of the Seas every man in the Hall scrambled upright and tried to look full of energy and totally untouched by the day's efforts. But Harald Blogfeld didn't appear to notice.

It was my father's place to put the contestants out of their misery.

"So, honoured guest," he said to Blogfeld. "You have seen our young men compete, and now the games are over. Can you tell us who has been chosen?"

This is it! I thought, and my mouth went dry. *This is when he tells us who it's going to be! Will it be Karl? What's he waiting for? Why doesn't he say? Get on with it!*

"Hmm?" said Blogfeld.

My father looked a little surprised. "We want to know who you've *chosen*," he said, a little louder this time.

"Chosen?" murmured Blogfeld. "Eh?" And for some reason, that word made the Widow *giggle*.

We all looked at each other in bewilderment. Where was Blogfeld's storm-at-sea voice? Where were his flashing eyes and booming laugh?

"Oh! Oh yes, I've chosen," he went on, with a very silly grin. "I've chosen... the finest woman in all the land."

"What?" cried half the Hall.

"Who?" cried the other half.

"This dear lady and I are going to be married. As soon as possible. If not sooner." And Blogfeld turned to the Widow and smiled in a *really* embarrassing way. She simpered back.

I turned to look at my father. He seemed to

have forgotten it was his job as host of the Games to get the great man back on topic. I don't think I've ever seen a more relieved, ecstatic look on a person's face before. Brownhilde wasn't after *him* any more. He'd been saved!

But those who hadn't just been reprieved from a ghastly fate had other things on their minds.

"But who have you chosen *to take raiding* with you?" cried one of the contestants. They were all crowding forward now.

"Tell us!" shouted another. "We have to know – *who won the Games*?"

Harald Blogfeld, Champion of the Waves, Scourge of the Seas, the Viking's Viking, paused and looked around vaguely.

"Won?" he said dreamily. "Who won?"

"*Yes!* Who won the games? Who have you chosen to take raiding with you?"

"Raiding?" He actually sounded puzzled by the word. "Oh no, not this year. I'm not thinking of any raiding this season. In fact, I don't expect

I'll be going raiding again. Ever. So I guess that means, um, you *all* won. Congratulations!"

There was a silence you could have cut with a blunt axe. It was wall-to-wall goggling eyes and dropped jaws. I know I must have looked just as gob-smacked as the rest of them. But Blogfeld and the Widow didn't appear to notice. In fact, they didn't seem to be aware of anything at all, except each other.

Yeurchhh!

As they wandered out into the night again, they passed quite close to where I was standing. Blogfeld was gazing at the Widow Brownhilde. There was a look on his face that for some reason made me think of puppies.

"I feel as if I've died and gone to Valhalla," he murmured huskily. "You are my Valkyrie."

I waited for the Widow to slug him one right across the ear, but it didn't happen. It should have. It so should have. But it didn't.

She just giggled.

"Would you look at that?" muttered my granny, suddenly appearing at my elbow. "She knew our Karl was going to be the Champion, so she nobbled the judge. Still, if I were forty years younger, I might have done the same. I'd have given her a run for her money!"

I smiled down into her wizened little face, thinking, *And you would have, at that!*

CHAPTER EIGHT

From Frondell with Love

Next day, our visitors packed their tents and their families back into their ships and sailed away with the tide. The last to go were the Widow Brownhilde (though we wouldn't be calling her *that* for much longer) and the ex-Scourge of the Seas. Blogfeld must have somehow inveigled the secret of the boar out of Queue, for, as they moved off, an extremely convincing billow of fire and smoke shot out of the dragon-prow's mouth, and everybody cheered. The two ships made a pretty picture as they glided down the fjord towards the open sea.

The Games were over for another year.

"That *was* fun!" my granny cackled cheerfully. Then she went off to tell my sisters the best way to clear up.

Karl watched the two ships until they were only dots in the distance. He still looked as if he'd been kicked in the stomach by a cow, but I figured he'd get over it. And I can't remember when I last saw my father looking so contented. He wandered about happily, lending a hand with the trestle tables, thanking people for all their hard work, making encouraging noises and generally being nice to everyone who came within range.

And then he spotted me.

"Leif," he said.

"Yes, father?"

"Do you remember our conversation earlier?
When you offered to chop off the Widow
Brownhilde's head and bring it to me on a
platter? Don't think I didn't notice how hard
you tried to keep her away from me all day – so
hard, in fact, that she ended up leaving with a
completely different husband." He gave me a
slap on the back that nearly knocked me over.
"Thank you, my boy, thank you! I don't know
how you did it – I don't understand half the

things that happened here yesterday – but I *do* know you did a champion's work!"

And if there had been a competition right then and there for which of us had the bigger grin ... well, I think it would have been a tie.